Rabbit Rabbits On

Susanna Gretz

Methuen Children's Books

Rabbit is boasting.
"I know how to do lots of tricks," he says.

"Like what?" asks Duck.
"What tricks?" asks Frog.

"Like . . . make chocolate sandwiches," says Rabbit.
"That's not a trick," says Duck.
"Anyone can do that," says Frog.

"Well, I also know how to do balancing," says Rabbit.
"I can balance all my sandwiches on my nose."
"Go on, then," says Duck.

"I can't do it now," explains Rabbit,
"because I've eaten all my sandwiches."
"Hmm," says Frog.

"Anyway," says Rabbit, "I also know how to do juggling."
"Go on, then," says Duck.

"I can't do it now," explains Rabbit,
"because I haven't got my juggling balls with me."
"Hmm, hmm," says Frog.
But Rabbit keeps rabbiting on.

"I can also throw a sandwich really high up," he says,
"and I can eat another one before it comes down!"
"I'll bet," says Duck.
"Go on, then," says Frog.

"Well," explains Rabbit, "I can't do it *now* –"
"Because you ate all your sandwiches," says Duck.
"That's right," says Rabbit, "*and* I've hurt my paw."

"I don't believe you," says Duck.

"Load of twaddle," says Frog. "Let's all go on the see-saw."

"OK," says Rabbit.

But Rabbit is heavier than Frog and Duck . . .

. . . so they soar high up in the air.
"I don't like this," says Frog. "I'm scared."

Then Duck has an idea.
"Let us down for a minute," she tells Rabbit. "It's a surprise."
Rabbit loves surprises. "OK," he says.
He lets them down and hides his eyes.

"Nearly ready," says Frog.
"Is it a nice surprise?" asks Rabbit.

"No peeking," says Duck.

"Surprise!" says Frog.
But now Rabbit is scared.
"Let me *down*!" he shouts.
"No!" yells Duck.

"Please!" calls Rabbit.

"If we let you down, will you stop making things up?"
asks Frog.

"I didn't make *everything* up," says Rabbit.
"What didn't you make up?"
"Well, I didn't make up the chocolate sandwiches,"
says Rabbit.

"You're sure?" asks Frog. She's feeling peckish.
Duck feels peckish too.
"If we let you down, will you promise not to make things up?"
Rabbit promises.

"We could go to your house, Rabbit," says Duck.

"And you could show us how to make chocolate sandwiches," says Frog.

So they did.